Androcles and the Lion

Based on a story by Aesop

Retold by
Russell Punter

Illustrated by

Mike and Carl Gordon

Reading Consultant: Alison Kelly
Roehampton University

A long time ago, there was a man called Androcles*.

He was very poor...

but he was kind.

*say And-rock-lees

Androcles worked for a rich man named Brutus[*].

Brutus lived in a big house outside the city of Rome.

*say Broo-tus

Brutus made his slaves
work hard. Every day,
Androcles scrubbed
steps...

mopped
floors...

Mop faster!

made beds...

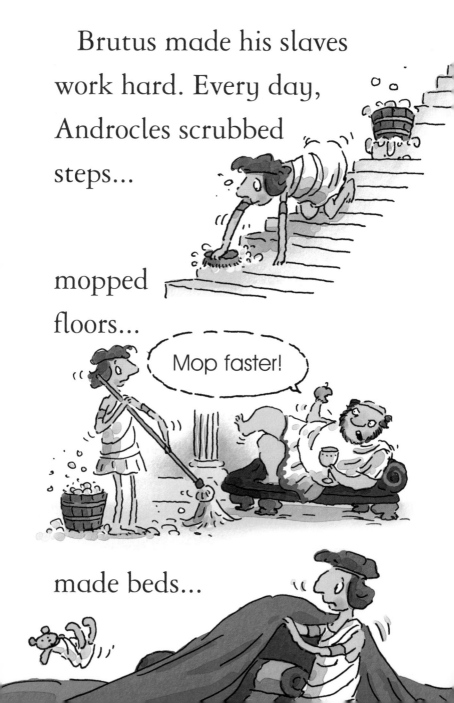

But Brutus never paid him.
All Androcles got was one
piece of dry bread a day.

One night, Androcles decided to run away. He climbed through a window.

Then he ran into the forest.

Androcles had never been in the forest before. It was dark and spooky.

Suddenly, he heard a loud
noise from behind a bush.

RAAAAGGGGGH!

Androcles jumped. "Who...
who's there?" he asked.

He looked around the bush
and saw...

RAAAAGGGGH!

an **enormous** lion.
Androcles ran.

But the lion didn't run
after Androcles. He sat there,
as still as stone.

Androcles was surprised.
He went back. "Why didn't
you chase me?" he asked.

"I can't run," sniffed the
lion. "I can't even walk.
There's a thorn in my paw."

"You poor thing," said
Androcles. "Let me help."

12

He gripped the thorn.
"This might hurt."

I can't look.

Androcles pulled out the
thorn, as quickly as he could.

"Oooch!" yelped the lion.
"All done," said Androcles.

"Thank you!" cried the lion
happily. "I'm Leo."

He smiled and gave
Androcles a big, sloppy lick.

Silluuuurp!

From then on, Androcles
and Leo were best friends.

They lived in a cave in the middle of the forest.

They hunted for food every day,

and, each night, they shared it.

One morning, Androcles
saw a stranger.

He tip-toed closer.

"A soldier!" he thought.
"What does he want?"

The soldier unrolled some
paper. Androcles gasped.

18

Just then, Androcles felt a
bug on his nose. It tickled.

"Hey!" cried the soldier.
"Stop right there!"

The soldier pulled out
his sword.

Androcles ran.

The soldier chased
Androcles between
bushes...

up hills...

down hills...

22

across a stream...

around
trees...

and out of
the forest.

Androcles got so tired,
he had to stop.

23

The soldier threw Androcles
into a cart.

"Are you taking me back to
Brutus?" panted Androcles.

"No," boomed the soldier.
"You're going to Rome."

"Why?" asked Androcles.
"You'll see," the soldier said.

Androcles had a bumpy
ride to Rome. The city was
crowded and noisy.

He had never seen so many people.

Then he noticed a big, round building. "What's that?" he asked.

"It's the arena*," said the soldier. "That's where you're going."

28

*say a-ree-na

"What happens there?"
asked Androcles.

"You'll see," the soldier said.

29

A man called Clinkus
pulled Androcles off the cart.

He led Androcles into the
arena, past a cage of lions.

They weren't as gentle
as Leo.

ROAR! SNARL!

Yikes!

"Why are they here?"
Androcles asked nervously.
"You'll see," said Clinkus.

Androcles was locked in
a prison with a man called
Marco.

"What happens now?"
asked Androcles.

"We fight in the arena,"
said Marco.

"But I don't want to fight you," said Androcles.

"We don't fight each other..." Marco sighed.

"We fight the lions."

Androcles gulped.

We'll be torn to pieces!

"Everyone in Rome comes to watch," said Marco. "Even the Emperor."

"Our fights are tomorrow afternoon," he added.

Androcles and Marco didn't get much sleep that night.

The next afternoon,
Clinkus dragged Androcles
from the prison.

He took him down a long,
dark tunnel to a doorway.

Clinkus pushed Androcles
through the door.

Androcles stood in the
middle of the arena.

Thousands of people sat around him. They gave a huge cheer.

Bring on the lion!

A gate opened in a side wall, and an **enormous** lion charged out.

Androcles trembled with
fear. There was
nowhere to run.

Androcles closed his eyes.
"I hope it's over quickly,"
he thought.

Then something strange
happened...

Androcles felt a lick on his hand. He opened his eyes to see... Leo!

Hello Androcles!

"I was caught last night," said Leo. "They brought me here to fight."

Androcles hugged his friend.
The crowd couldn't believe it.

"Androcles has tamed the lion," they cried. "What a hero!"

Clinkus took Androcles to the Emperor.

"You were very brave,"
said the Emperor. "I think I'll
set you free."

Androcles thought of his
friends. "Please will you free
Marco and the lion too?"

The Emperor smiled.
"Very well," he said.

My hero!

Androcles and his friends
left Rome and started their
own show.

And no one had to fight.

Androcles and the Lion is based on one of Aesop's Fables. These are a collection of short stories, told in Greece about 4,000 years ago. The stories always have a moral (a message or lesson) at the end. The moral of this story is: be kind to your friends and they will never forget you.

Series editor: Lesley Sims

First published in 2008 by Usborne Publishing Ltd., Usborne House, 83-85 Saffron Hill, London EC1N 8RT, England. www.usborne.com
Copyright © 2008 Usborne Publishing Ltd.